ASKING THE RIVER

ASKING THE RIVER

A NOVEL BY DAVID KHERDIAN

ILLUSTRATED BY
NONNY HOGROGIAN

ORCHARD BOOKS   NEW YORK

Orchard Books
95 Madison Avenue
New York, NY 10016

Manufactured in the United States of America
Book design by Nonny Hogrogian
The text of this book is set in 12 point Palatino.
The illustrations are drawn in pencil.
1   3   5   7   9   10   8   6   4   2

Library of Congress Cataloging-in-Publication Data
Kherdian, David.
Asking the river / by David Kherdian; illustrated by
Nonny Hogrogian.
p.   cm.
Summary: While trying to make it through elementary
school in Racine, Wisconsin, a thirteen-year-old Armenian
American boy must come to terms with his heritage, his
parents' expectations, and his own uncertainty about
what he wants from life.
ISBN 0-531-05483-7.   ISBN 0-531-08633-X (lib. bdg.)
[1. Armenian Americans—Fiction.   2. Immigrants—Fiction.
3. Identity—Fiction.]   I. Hogrogian, Nonny, ill.   II. Title.
PZ7.K527As   1993   [Fic]—dc20   92-34912

For Nonny

BOOK ONE

GARFIELD SCHOOL

I was staring out the window at the playground below. It was deserted, where just moments before we had all been shouting and playing. Now we were cooped up in our classroom, which for me was a prison. It was a prison for all of us who felt unwanted. Not just the other Armenian kids like me, but anyone whose parents were foreign, or any of those who thought of themselves as something other than American. Like the Jews, Greeks, and Italians, for instance. We envied the Americans—as everyone else excepting the blacks was called— and we would have liked to be Americans our- selves, but not if it meant giving up whatever else we were.

I was listening to the clanking of milk bottles and garbage cans. I looked out the window again.

Our playground was backed by the buildings on State Street. The raised voices of the women in the tenements carried across the yard. We were on the same level, but they were far enough away that I couldn't hear their talk. One of them was shaking out her mop and talking to her neighbor, who was hanging clothes on the line. She turned now and leaned on her mop and stared up at the sky. I wondered what was going through her mind.

"Steven," Miss Ransard called. I turned and looked at her, even though my name isn't Steven. My name is Stepan Bakaian, or Step for short. I've been called Bak also, which isn't as cool, but it's better than Steven, which is my "American" name, given to me in the first grade by that old battle-ax Swanson. That's the grade when all the foreign kids got their American names.

I looked down at my copy of the Fifth Reader, which Miss Ransard was holding open in front of her. She was staring at me over the top of the cracked spine, her bifocals about to slide off her delicate nose. "Yes," I said grudgingly.

"*Well*," she said, dragging out the word until the room filled with her voice as well as with her impatience and contempt for me. "We were reading about how the barbarians stormed the gates of China and nearly toppled an empire, and how, as a result, they caused the erection of the Great Wall of China, one of the monumental achievements of Man. Don't you care about what Man has *done*? Don't you find this *fascinating*?"

4

I stared back at her, but I didn't answer the statement she pretended was a question. I was thinking to myself that the only thing fascinating about what she had said was that it was the first time I could remember any of my teachers mentioning the Chinese. All we ever got was American history and European history. I don't think there was one word in any of the books we were taught from about the Armenians. All the Americans ever said about us was that we were the starving Armenians, which in their minds was anything but fascinating. They talked about us as if we didn't really exist—like we were so far away in their minds that we were nowhere at all. Well, those starving Armenians happened to be my relatives. My own aunt was one of them, or she would have been my aunt if she hadn't starved to death before I was born. That was my father's sister. But it was even worse for my mom. She lost everybody, and not just from starvation alone, but from cholera, dysentery, and outright murder. This was during World War I, when the Turks tried to get rid of all the Armenians living in their country.

I wanted to tell her to ram the Chinese wall up her fat ass. But I didn't. I had already flunked the second grade once, and the fifth grade twice—once during the regular year, and again at the summer session. Grade school had become a jail sentence, and all I wanted was to get through it and move on to junior high, where it might be different.

I looked from Miss Ransard to the clock on the wall, considering what to say. I couldn't help but notice that I was being stared at by everyone in the room. Some of my classmates were looking at me with pity and others with scorn, but the Armenian kids only looked embarrassed.

The bell rang in the hallway, announcing the end of class. "All right, children," Miss Ransard said, "put your books away neatly, stand up, and file out. We're going across the hall to Room Ten for your first music lesson with Miss Schultz. Be alert and attentive, now. Make me proud of you."

ROOT RIVER

I had taken my bike out of the rack and I was absentmindedly bouncing the front tire up and down on the pavement, while cursing Miss Ransard under my breath. Several boys were circling the large elm tree in the school yard and calling out teasing remarks to the girls as they walked by. I turned my bike around and headed for the back gate.

I pretended to be invisible as I rode up State Street to Forest, and then down Liberty Street to Island Park. I didn't know where I was going and I didn't want to know. I circled the park twice. It was deserted except for two old men sitting on one of the benches above the winding river.

I was getting ready to cross back over the Liberty Street bridge and head for home, but I changed my mind at the last minute. Instead of dismounting, I rode up to the cement railing that came up to my waist and seated myself on the bridge while holding on to my bike with my feet. In the yard facing the park was a rock garden that imitated in miniature the bridge I was sitting on. I wondered who the man was that had made the rock garden. It had always fascinated me, and I had never walked across the bridge without stopping to look at it.

I lowered my eyes from the garden to the river below and watched it turn out of my sight around the bend beyond the park on its way to Lake Michigan, where its brown waters would enter the life of the great blue lake.

I lowered myself onto my bike and headed up the hill, taking the back streets and alleys to my home. I entered our backyard by riding through our neighbor's yard, which was on the street behind ours. I parked my bike against the rear of our house, facing the garden and grape arbor built by the German family who lived here before we did. It wasn't something my father could have built.

My mom was in the kitchen preparing supper. I walked to the ice box and dished some yogurt into a saucer.

"Hello, *yavroos*," she said.

"Hello, Mom." I sprinkled some sugar over my yogurt and sat down at the table. I was watching my mother's fingertips as she spread out a grape leaf. She sprinkled some water on the filling before placing a portion of ground lamb and rice into the spread leaf, turning in the two ends, and rolling it into a perfect cylinder.

"You didn't come straight home," she said without looking up from her work. "In the Old Country it was horses, and in the new country it's bikes and autos. It is the same, yes? Men like to go out. They like to come home, but not before they've gone out. Your father came all the way to America—do you know why?" She paused without looking up from her work. "So he could go home again, buy a white horse, and ride over his newly purchased land, a *pasha*. You didn't know that."

"No," I said, "I didn't know that."

She wiped a hair from her forehead with her wrist and then dipped her fingers in the water glass before sprinkling the filling. "You see, you are not so different from your father."

"I'm an American."

"You are also an Armenian."

"Yes," I admitted, "an Armenian-American. That's what everyone tells me."

"You're grumbling again. Now what is it?"

"I'm one thing inside—myself—but on the out-side I'm these two things, and I don't know what either one is supposed to be."

My mother stopped her work to look at me. "So what! Is it something terrible? Are you being tortured? Have they taken your passport away?"

"What passport?" I shouted.

"Shut up and eat your yogurt."

"I don't have to shut up."

"Listen to me. I want you to be a proud Armenian. We are a great people with a great history. We were the first nation to adopt Christianity."

"Yeah, and before that we worshiped fire, right?"

She ignored the question. "We are older and wiser than the Americans. They have no common sense. Look how they live. Look how they raise their children—like chickens, any which way. If you want to know, that's how you are an American: you have no common sense."

"You and your common sense. If the Armenians had any common sense, they would have gotten out of Turkey and not gotten themselves massacred."

"That's finished. Now we are in America. Our back is turned from that."

"What are you talking about? That's all any of you think about. Whenever there's an earthquake in Turkey, you rejoice. Our biggest heroes are martyrs. Our holidays celebrate battle scenes and death. Defeat, defeat, defeat—"

"We have hope. And our hope is you. Don't forget your *jeentz*. You are here. Fine! You're an American. That's good! I'm happy! But you come from somewhere else. You can have a great future—here in America. *Your* America. But you already have a great past—that was prepared for you in advance. We didn't suffer for nothing. We suffered for *you*! You're our hope!" She looked down at the grape leaf spread in front of her and quickly rolled it and placed it in the cooking pan.

"And what am I supposed to do in America?"

"It doesn't matter. Whatever you choose. First you will be educated, and then we will see. With your *jarbeek* you will change America."

"It takes more than genes and enterprise," I said. "How about pull, influence, and being in the right place at the right time with the right people? I don't see the Armenians putting on a show with their *jeentz* and their *jarbeek*."

"What show?" My mother looked up from her work and scowled at me. "This is not a radio program. This is life, not a movie. You will see. One generation, two generations—we will make even America rich."

"Ma, for crying out loud, they don't even want us here."

"What are you saying? This is the land of promise, of hope. This country is our salvation. They took us in. They sheltered us. We have made a home here, a community, everything!"

"But we're not Americans."

"Thank God!"

"Ma, what are you saying?"

"We're American enough."

"Enough for you maybe, but not enough for me."

NICKY TEKEYAN

Every time I had one of these discussions with my mom, I had to get out of the house in a hurry. I slammed the door to let her know how I felt. But instead of getting on my bike, I walked down the rickety stairs at the end of our dead-end block and headed for my friend Nicky's house. I walked up Prospect Street and turned the corner at La Salle. High above my head a redheaded woodpecker was hammering away at one of the trees I had just walked under. I got a glimpse of him, but when I moved around the tree to have a better look, he just circled ahead of me while climbing higher and higher in the tree. "Come back," I hollered, as if he could understand English. But he kept climbing higher. "*Yegour,*" I said again, this time in Armenian, and he disappeared from sight.

I kicked a pebble along the ground, trying to see if I could keep it on the sidewalk, so it would be a game. It lasted for six squares before ricocheting into the grass. I hurried up the street with my head down, hoping to find something usable, like a discarded pack of cigarettes so I could add to my tinfoil collection. When I came to the Tekeyans', I walked in the front door and peered into the living room. Lily was sitting by herself on the couch, listening to a Duke Ellington record. Eva was in the dining room, ironing. Arpey, Avak, and Nicky were nowhere in sight. "Nicky's on the upstairs porch," Lily said, "trying out his new airplane."

"Thanks," I said, and bounded up the stairs. When I opened the door to the porch, Nicky was winding the propeller on his latest model airplane. "Hi ya, Step," he said.

"Wait up," I called. "Let me have a look at your plane before you set it off. I don't want to miss out on the crash."

"Don't say that—you'll bring me bad luck. Not that anything could go wrong, of course."

"What do you mean?" I said. "You always crash them—sooner or later."

"It ain't inevitable, you know. It's just a matter of time before I perfect my technique and make one that will never crash."

"Fat chance," I said. "Even if nothing gets in its way, like that wall out there, you can't count on a perfect landing."

"That's what I'm working on. If the weight distribution is just right, it won't ever crash."

"Well, you've got a good day for it," I conceded. There weren't any kids playing in the empty lot next to Nicky's house, which I knew was the reason he was out flying.

"I'm not like you," Nicky said, "wanting to fly planes through the trees or setting them on fire before takeoff, hoping they'll burn up in midair and come crashing down in a trail of smoke, like in the movies. Not that you've built a plane since I can remember."

"I'm saving my money for better things," I said, "but I like watching you send yours off. Anyhow, I wish there was a way to figure out how to get the pilot out safely by parachute once the plane goes up in smoke. That would really be something."

"It won't ever happen. The genius who could figure out how to do that with a toy would put his energy into something constructive."

"Well, he wouldn't if he were twelve years old."

"Yeah, but there aren't any twelve-year-old geniuses that I've heard of."

"How about sailing it through the trees?" I said. "Just to try your luck. Maybe it'll get through unscratched."

I figured with Nicky's luck he could make it. Maybe. But he wasn't into luck; he was into figuring out how things worked. Luck was a by-product of his curiosity was how Lily explained it to me one day. Lily understood everything.

Nicky's plane was wound up and ready to go. "Okay, Buckeye," he said, "three and a half loops to a perfect landing. Go ahead and do your stuff." Old Buckeye made a loop and a dive, then arched into a long, sweeping flight that I was afraid would take it into the street. But it seemed to put on the brakes at the last second and came down just short of the sidewalk in front of the street.

"Perfection," Nicky hollered. "See that, Step? Isn't she a beaut?"

We raced down the steps and out the door. "Let's try her again," I said.

"Not today, Step. I want to revel in the glory of my ace here for at least twenty-four hours."

"See you tomorrow, then," I said. I laughed. "Should I bring my matches?" But Nicky didn't even hear me. He was holding his plane up, shoulder high and in mock flight, while imitating the sound of a humming engine as he headed back across the lot.

WILLY SPRINGER

It was Friday afternoon—at last. The first week of school was over. I had come straight home from class and I was in my room sorting out my baseball cards when I heard Willy Springer's truck pull up outside. The Springers were our next-door neighbors. Willy worked in Chicago as a photoengraver. He was also a drummer for a pickup band that played for weddings and practiced every Wednesday night in their parlor. But best of all Willy was a fisherman who fished with nets—not like the ordinary fishermen who used cane poles. He seined Root River for bait, and he used nets on Lake Michigan to catch perch and herring and lake trout. I always dreamed that he would take me out on his boat one day, but so far I hadn't been asked. I was too proud to ask, or even hint that I wanted to go out with him.

When he pulled up in his truck instead of his old jalopy, it meant that he had been to the lake. I could hear the raised voices from my room, including his nephews'. They lived the next street over.

I walked outside to our grape arbor, sat down, and waited for them to back the truck between our homes to their backyard, where they would begin hauling out the boxes loaded with their nets and their catch.

I could see my father through the grape leaves, barefoot as usual, hoeing among the weeds. All that was left of his summer crop were some tubers and a patch of Swiss chard that was nearly two and a half feet high and came up to his waist, from where I was sitting. He wanted my mom to use the Swiss chard for *sarma*, but she always refused, preferring the traditional grape leaves she was used to. He called to me to come and have a look at his garden, but I didn't answer. He gestured again, pointing to the ground at something he wanted me to come and have a look at. I made a face and turned away.

Just then, Willy's son, Freddie, came bounding out of the house to join the men in the yard. They were poling the nets and throwing the squirming fish into boxes, dividing them by size. Willy's nephews, Frank and Bobby—my playmates—began cleaning the fish while the two men, Willy and his cousin Charley, worked at the nets. Freddie went down the basement stairs at the rear of their house and soon returned with a block of ice hoisted over his right shoulder by pincers, like the regular icemen used.

With his ice pick in hand, he quickly began chipping pieces into one of the rectangular boxes. Frank and Bobby worked as a team. Frank grabbed one of the living perch, banged its head on the side of the boxboard, instantly scaled it, and then tossed it to Bobby, who slit the stomach open and, cutting off the head, slid the guts out in a piece. He tossed the cleaned fish into Freddie's box of ice.

Just as soon as Freddie had enough fish to fill an order, he covered the load with a gunnysack and went riding off to one of the taverns that had a standing order with the Springers. All of the taverns in Racine that had kitchens specialized in Friday night fish fries.

While all this was going on, Willy's scroungy cats were wailing for fish heads and guts. They kept edging closer, meowing plaintively. Bobby enjoyed peppering them with his fish heads. After jumping and screeching, they'd rush back in a pack and pounce on the dirt-covered heads and guts.

Willy's dog, Bozo, was racing madly about. The excitement of howling cats, working men, and jumping fish crashing against the boxes was driving him crazy. But no one, least of all the cats, paid any attention to him.

I was dying to walk over and have a look at the fish, especially the herring, because they were seldom caught off the pier, and also the trout, which could only be caught with nets, as they ran deep and never came near shore.

I had been sitting on the round table in the arbor, with my feet on the bench. I stood up now to have a better look, being careful not to be seen. If I couldn't be a part of something myself, I liked looking in on it without being noticed.

"Hey there, sonny," Willy called out to me. He had spotted me without my noticing. "The perch are running. Yessiree Bob, running to beat the band. Ask the boys here."

Willy Springer called all the boys in the neighborhood sonny, and the girls sis.

"You know what they say, 'When the wind's from the south, it blows the bait into the fish's mouth.'" He licked a finger and stuck it up in the air. "Sure enough!" he pronounced, laughing to himself and giving a wink and a clap followed by a little bend and half step, which was his routine and trademark whenever he was feeling happy about something.

If I had thought about it, I would have known that what he was happy about was the catch they had made, the money he would soon be taking in, and—this being Friday night—the time he would have on the town with his wife, Matty. But I took the wink as being for me, for the running fish, and also for the sheer joy of fishing—in this case, *good* fishing—that he was letting me in on.

I jumped down from the bench, reached under the table for my pail, and then took a pole down from the rain spout below the slope of our roof.

"Goin' to the pier," I shouted to my mom through the kitchen window that looked out on our backyard.

"Take one of these perch for fish bait," Willy said. "You won't need anything else."

I shooed Bozo with my pole, without having any effect on his barking, and looked down at the wash bucket of breathing, squirming fish. Willy picked out a medium-sized perch and dropped it in my bucket.

JOE PERCH

I hurried down the rickety stairs of our dead-end block onto the street below, which led to the lake. Ours was the second to last house on the block, and the Springers' was the last. I always rode to Root River, but to Lake Michigan I walked—and not just because it was a lot closer, but because there wasn't a safe place to park my bike near the pier, and I didn't want to invest in a tire guard. I had better things to spend my money on. Also, I liked to walk because of the factories near the lake that I would have to wind my way through. I sometimes found useful junk.

But an even better reason was the tiny park halfway between our house and the lake, which contained a tiny fountain. I always stopped there for a long drink of water. I liked the damp smell, and while I drank I'd stare past the perforated brass ball at the white and brown pebbles of stone.

From the factories I could hear the blast of the foghorn at the end of the pier. I hurried my step. I could see the masts of the sailboats. The smell of the lake was in my nostrils. As I passed the marina and headed up the pier, I cast my eyes down at the filthy brown water on the harbor side of the lake. It was polluted with condoms, bottles, and the refuse spewed up from the city sewers, as well as bloated fish. The contrast was startling, for the water on the other side of the pier was blue and clear and good enough to drink.

One of the thrills that went with fishing on the pier was stopping on the way out to watch Joe Perch, and also to admire his catch. He was the master fisherman of the pier and always had a stringer full of perch, whether or not the fish were biting for anyone else. The thing that made him different, right off, was that he fished close in, where the water was no more than five or six feet deep. The pier was shored up at this point with huge white boulders that were clearly visible.

The only thing Joe Perch had in common with the rest of us was that he used cane poles—not one or two, like us, but three. Except for his imitators, he was the only one on the pier to use bobbers, and not just ordinary store-bought bobbers, but wine bottle corks fastened to his lines with matchsticks. Also, he didn't put any sinkers on his lines, nor did he ever switch bait, like we did—from crab tails to minnows to worms to fish bait and then back again. No, he fished exclusively with minnows, and not hooked through the back and head, but *under* the back and below the spine, so they would stay alive. He would ease them carefully into the water, and every now and then, when the waves churned against the rocks, you could see one of his minnows floating toward the surface, swimming gamefully.

"Hot dog," I shouted. I had stopped in front of Joe Perch and was staring down at his stringer of fish. "Wowie, Joe, some fishing!" Joe Perch didn't bother to turn around. He was all business when it came to fishing.

I continued walking out to my spot at the end of the pier. I could see for myself that no one else was having any luck. Willy had tricked me again. The fish weren't biting.

I caught three small perch and quit. But I didn't really care, because about the time I was getting ready to quit I remembered it was Friday, and that meant payday. I could hear J. I. Case's whistle toot in the distance, which meant the day shift was over. The logo for Case was an eagle, and the workers liked to say that the eagle shit on Friday, which meant they would be getting paid.

And Friday night for me meant shoeshining with a friend, a chance to make some money of my own. So it was a kind of payday for me also.

"Never mind," my mother said when I walked into the kitchen with my embarrassing catch. "What did you expect?"

"How come I can't learn that the fish are never biting when Willy says they are?"

"Because you want to believe him. Also you know he isn't necessarily lying. Exaggerating maybe, but not lying. He wants you to catch fish, and he enjoys seeing you go off. . . ."

"But why can't I learn my lesson?"

"Because you're a dreamer, like Willy. You hope they're biting instead of determining for yourself whether they are biting or not."

"No one can know that, Mom, for crumb's sake. The only way to find out is to go to the pier."

"Then what are you complaining about? You went—they weren't biting. Next time you go, they'll bite."

"No they won't."

"Shut up and wash your hands and face. Then you can eat. Your food is warming on the stove."

I walked past my dad, who was sitting in the dining room. He was smoking a cigarette and listening to the news on the radio. It was Gabriel Heater, shouting about the war. My dad clucked at me without looking up. As usual, his teeth were missing. He wore them to work, but he took them out as soon as he came home. He was probably resting his gums until it was time to eat. If I had caught a mess of fish, I would have bragged to him, but since I hadn't it was best not to say anything so I wouldn't get teased.

I walked into my room and closed the door.

KIRK OHANIAN

My best friend at Garfield was Kirk. We were the same age and the stars of the basketball and softball teams. He was also my neighbor. It was a ritual for us to go shoeshining together on Friday night.

I picked up my shoeshine box and headed for his house by going down the stairs at the end of our dead-end street, and then up the hill on the worn path of the empty lot between Prospect Street and Jackson Street, where Kirk lived. Our houses were at eye level and nearly straight across from each other. Jackson Street was off Douglas Avenue, one of the better streets for shoeshining because of all the bars.

Our parents had accepted this latest craze of ours to make money for the things we wanted that our families couldn't afford to get for us. However, there was such a thing as *ahmoht,* and there was also such a thing as pride, and shoeshining made me question certain things I wasn't dying to look at.

There was something humiliating about shining shoes in a bar. I don't know if everyone felt that way, but I'm pretty sure all the Armenian kids did.

I didn't want to do anything that made me feel inferior. It was bad enough to be made to feel that way when I was in school, but there I didn't have a choice.

Kirk's dad worked at Belle City Foundry and had an even worse job than my dad's; my dad was a sweeper at J. I. Case. The foundries were hot, dirty, and dangerous. I don't know if it was because of the long hours he spent at work, or if it was because of Wisconsin's cold climate, but he was always complaining of drafts when he was at home. "Woman," he'd call to Kirk's mom, "again a draft has entered the room."

Mrs. Ohanian would come out of the kitchen and stand in the doorway, looking worried and confused. Without saying a word, she'd rush back into the kitchen and either bring him a cup of tea or a shawl for his shoulders. He'd sigh and then look up into her face, to see if his suffering had taken its proper effect on her.

I didn't like to spend any more time than was necessary at Kirk's house, so I usually stood by the kitchen door and waited for him to get ready.

Once we were safely out of his house, we began walking up Jackson Street toward Douglas

Avenue. Kirk began talking about how well he thought we would do. "I feel like we ought to make a dollar each. Let's shoot for it, okay, Step?" I nodded my agreement and looked over at Kirk, who was feeling as anxious and nervous as I was about entering our first tavern of the night.

"The important thing is not to be too pushy," Kirk said.

"Where does that come from?" I said, because it didn't sound like it came from him.

"That's what Miss Baker said to me last year when she flunked me. 'Pushy people don't get ahead' is how she put it. And then she said, 'Try to fit in.' Maybe it's good advice. We ought to give it a try if it helps us not to flunk."

"That's her opinion," I said. "Maybe if she stopped pushing us back, we'd stop pushing to get ahead. Anyhow, we're Armenians, and we couldn't behave like dried-up *odars* if we wanted to, which is what she is."

"No reason to be prejudiced about it," Kirk said.

"They started it," I said, "and unless they lay off, I'm going to finish it."

"Like heck you are. This ain't our country—it's theirs."

"It's as much ours as anybody's," I said, but I didn't believe it.

"Prove it," Kirk said.

"I don't have to," I said. "From now on when someone asks me my nationality, I'm going to say American."

27

"They'll only laugh at you."

"Well, it's technically correct," I said. "Nationality means the country of your birth, which is the country you are a citizen of. I looked it up."

"Well, forget it. You're an Armenian, and that's what you'll always be."

We turned left at the corner and headed up Douglas Avenue. It was dark out, and cold enough that we could see our breath against the night air. I looked out at the flashing neon lights of the taverns up ahead.

Taverns were scary at night. They were dark, smoke-filled, and often noisy, with people talking all the time and the jukebox going strong. They had a funny smell as well, kind of stale and putrid, probably because the doors and windows were never opened. That's why we worked as a pair. We needed each other's moral support just to go inside.

We walked through the door of Charley's Bar and Grill and stopped to let our eyes adjust to the dark. I held my shoe box up in front of me with both hands. I had inscribed on the side of my box "A Shine for a Dime." A couple of the drinkers at the end of the bar looked up at us and then turned away. I approached a couple sitting by themselves at the bar, while I noticed out of the corner of my eye that Kirk was heading for one of the tables where a card game was going on.

"Would the lady like a shine?" I asked the man. The woman looked over at the man and smiled. He slowly and reluctantly turned and looked at me.

28

He had high cheekbones and thin, mousy hair that fell unparted over his forehead. They didn't look married, so I felt I could count on a tip if the man said yes. "A shine for a dime," I offered.

"Go ahead, Doris," he allowed. "Give the little guy a break." He hadn't noticed that she had already shined her shoes for the evening. It was obvious that he had had enough to drink. She had a half-finished drink in front of her and a full one behind. His lone glass was empty.

"What school do you go to?" Doris said, extending her foot.

"Garfield," I muttered, reaching inside my box for brown Kiwi. She was wearing two-tone spectators. I would daub on the white liquid later, and if I was a little sloppy, it would be easier to remove my mistake with the tip of a clean rag over the new, greasy polish I was applying to the tips and heels.

"My son went to Garfield. He's at Washington Junior High now. Do you live on Liberty Street?" she asked. I could feel her staring down at my black, wavy hair. All of the homes on the first block of Liberty were occupied by Armenian families.

I said, "Uh-uh, Superior Street, ma'am."

I hated being talked to this way. I wished I had worn a hat. That way, if she looked down on my head, she wouldn't see me, but a piece of fabric. Maybe I'd inscribe something on it, like "How would you know?" or "Not if the weather changes." Anything to get the attention off myself.

"You're going to like Washington Junior," she said.

"I'm going to like leaving Garfield," I said.

"I can tell you don't like it," she said. She had probably heard that the foreign kids were often flunked at Garfield Elementary.

She nudged her escort. "He's going to be happy to leave Garfield, Marvin. And probably the other one, too." She was looking over at Kirk, who had gotten a shine at one of the tables.

Marvin pretended he hadn't heard her. He was fingering his change on the bar when he realized that his glass was empty. He called to the bartender by rattling the remaining ice cubes in his glass. Doris reached in her purse and slipped me a quarter, as if it was a secret between us. It was a dime more than I expected, but I wasn't all that grateful under the circumstances.

We were standing on the sidewalk under the streetlight in front of Tony's Tap, trying to enjoy the night air and looking up at a family of moths banging their stupid heads against the molded glass of the twin lights above our heads. We were considering which bar to hit next. "Did you feel *ahmoht* in there?" Kirk said.

"Why do you ask that?" I said. "There's nothing *ahmoht* about shining shoes."

"I know there's not," Kirk said, "but still, you know what I mean."

"If you don't brood on it, then it doesn't matter."

"I'm saving up for a football, right? You're saving up for a .22 rifle, right?"

"Right!"

"That's it, then. Forget it."

"It's forgotten," I said. "But what do you think would happen if an Armenian woman went into one of their taverns?"

"She'd be shipped back to the Old Country, I guess. Why, what do you think would happen?"

"I don't know," I said. "It wouldn't happen. I don't know why I thought of it."

"Why should we feel *ahmoht*, anyhow? It's stupid."

"Look how our dads have to work for a living."

"That's not *ahmoht*," Kirk said.

"Of course not. Who said it was?"

"I'm not working in no factory when I grow up."

"That makes two of us."

"What are you gonna do, then?"

"I like to draw," I said.

"Like Rembrandt, I suppose," Kirk said, and laughed. "What say we shine shoes till we've got three dollars between us, and if it ain't too late we can go shoot a couple games of pool at Ace Grill."

"It's a deal," I said.

ACE GRILL

I was watching Kirk line up the eight ball in the side pocket. It was a tough shot, but I was sure he would sink it, making it three games in a row. I had won the first game, at least. If this were the World Series of Pool, he'd have to win one more game before I won three straight in order to win the title. But it wasn't the World Series, it was a pickup game at Ace Grill, it was getting late, and three straight losses meant thirty cents out of my pocket. It was a good thing we weren't playing for anything on the side. The cost of the game was bad enough. But it was worth it, especially with school out for two whole days, and with a chance to make some extra money. I had just earned $1.65, and I could shine shoes again tomorrow night if I wanted. Saturday was movie day, and Sunday would be a pickup football game, or else I'd go over to the Tekeyans' and work on my scrapbook with Nicky.

The eight ball plopped into the side pocket, and I watched the cue ball bounce off the rails, hoping it would scratch. It didn't. I had to admit it: Kirk was the best. Not only at pool, but softball, football, basketball, and any other league game or pickup game we might think up. Not a lot better, but just better enough to be the undeclared champ. I was pretty darn good myself. In fact, we were one-two at all the team sports, and our team, Garfield, was the league champ in softball and basketball. And we figured to stay champs for the next two years.

We also had the oldest players in the league, which meant we were champs at flunking, too. Kirk and I were the stars, along with Harry Manoogian. Kirk had flunked three times to our two. Of course I didn't count flunking fifth twice, since it was the same grade, and the second time was summer school, so I only lost one year. We had already calculated how old we would be when we graduated from high school: Kirk twenty-one, me twenty, and Harry nineteen—but he would be twenty a month after graduation. At that rate it looked like we would be shaving before we even got out of grade school.

My mom was waiting up for me when I got home. I stopped in the doorway of the living room and looked in on her. She peered at me over her glasses, the lace doily she was making still in her hand. It was one of the things she was expert at. She made all her own presents to save money because my father made so little in the factory.

My mom didn't understand me, but she was the only person I had to talk to, aside from Lily, and occasionally my uncle Mihran. I definitely couldn't talk to my dad. "Hello, *yavroos*," she said. "Is everything all right?"

"Of course, Mom. What did you expect?"

She didn't answer. I don't think she knew what she wanted for me, except that I be happy and safe. I looked up from the doily in her hand to the painting behind her of Mt. Ararat, the symbol of the Armenian nation. I seemed to surprise her when I asked, "Are the Turks like us?"

"Of course not. What a question. They murdered our tiny nation."

"But do they look like us? You know what I mean."

"They are Moslems. We are Christians."

"But are they dark like us, or are they maybe even darker?"

"About the same—some darker, some lighter. They are a mixed-up race, not like us—pure!" My mother was darker than my father, and I took after her.

"So that wasn't it, then—they weren't prejudiced against us because we were different looking?"

"I told you—we were Christians."

"*That* was the prejudice?"

"Hatred! Discrimination!"

"We were aggressive, weren't we? Always trying to get ahead. Better than everyone else, always hustling."

"*Yavroos*, if you don't have your own country, it is harder, much harder. You can never understand. We were taxed, cheated, robbed. We had no rights in the courts. Nothing! We were violated. Someday you will understand. . . ."

"But we were the clever ones."

"We had to be."

And now it's happening here, I thought. In one way we'll always get by; in another way we'll never be equal. But I kept my mouth shut because my mother always defended America when we had these arguments. She didn't have to be an American, nor could she be an American, only a citizen of the United States. She was a foreigner. But I *was* an American, or rather an Armenian-American. Did being both make me neither? I wondered. Was that my nationality—neither? Is that why I was always uncomfortable with myself, with my parents, and also with the Americans?

"ALL OF ME"

I slept in, as I always did on the weekend. By the time I got up, my father had already gone grocery shopping. My mother was in the kitchen, cutting away the fat on a shoulder of lamb. She stopped what she was doing and made me *basturma* and eggs for breakfast. "Toast or *choreg*?" she asked.

"*Choreg*," I said.

"Tea or milk?"

"Milk—it's faster. I'm going to the Tekeyans' just as soon as I pack my extra baseball cards."

When I pulled up on my bike, Nicky was sitting on the porch, reading the *Sporting News*. "Arpey's playing 'All of Me,'" he said. I knew, of course, what he meant. Arpey could play the same song fifty times in a row and never grow tired of it. We walked inside together at the very moment that

36

Arpey was leaving the living room to go upstairs. The record had stopped playing but was still winding to a stop on the turntable. Avak walked into the room with one of those look-out-here-I-come grins on his face. He removed the record and placed it under the cushion of the chair Arpey had been sitting in.

Nicky and I walked into the kitchen. We could hear his mom stirring ice cubes into a new pitcher of lemonade—her specialty.

When we walked back into the living room with our glasses, Arpey was coming down the stairs. Lily and Eva were seated on the sofa, discussing the latest feature attraction at the Rialto Theater, and Avak had taken a chair in the corner of the room. He said very casually, "Arpey, don't sit down in that chair again." Arpey looked over at Avak and placed her hand on the arm of the club chair she had been sitting in. She smiled defensively.

"That's right," Eva said. "Don't sit in that chair."

"Why not?" Arpey said, still smiling.

"I wouldn't sit there if I were you," Nicky said.

"Not a good idea, Arpey," Avak said. "Don't do it."

Lily remained silent, calculating the scene and trying not to get involved.

Arpey took a step forward in front of the chair, pretending she was about to sit down.

"Uh-uh," Avak, Eva, and Nicky said in succession. "Better not, Arpey."

"Don't do it," I said, speaking for the first time and, like the others, not meaning a word of what I said.

"Why shouldn't I?" Arpey said. Her smile by now was turning into a grimace.

"Can't tell you," Avak said, "but I know you don't want to sit in that chair."

"I *do* want to," Arpey said.

"You *don't* want to," Nicky said.

"You don't know what I want," Arpey said.

"Oh, yes I do," Avak said, "all too well."

Arpey sat down, but so slowly and cautiously that for an instant nothing happened. But then, all at once, we heard the faint but unmistakable sound that only a splitting, cracking record can make.

Arpey sprang up from her chair. She didn't utter a word at first, but she had a terrible, ghastly look on her face. Then she slowly lifted the cushion and stared down at the shattered record.

"We told you not to sit down," Avak said—before being drowned out by her screams.

"We didn't do it, Arpey," Eva said. "*You* did it."

"Monsters, devils, beasts," Arpey screamed. "I hate all of you." She continued screaming as she ran up the stairs to her room.

"She'll get another one," Eva said.

"But not immediately," Avak said.

"That was great," Nicky said. "No question, she had it coming."

Lily was the only one who looked unhappy. She got up and walked to the stairs. Unlike her brothers and sisters, Lily had her own room. It wasn't long before she began playing her cello. She was saving up to go to Juilliard so she could become a classical musician. At least that's what everyone said. Lily never talked about it herself. She was very private, and also a loner, like me, which was probably why I liked her and also looked up to her.

I was visualizing Lily's bow moving across the strings of her cello. The music was sad but not in the least mournful. It kept growing in intensity without losing any of its softness. I could feel Lily's presence in the room over our heads, but when I looked up I realized that I was the only one listening to the music.

TYRONE POWER

Nicky had gone back to the porch with the *Sporting News* under his arm. Avak was in the kitchen, and Eva was ironing again in the living room. I walked outside and sat next to Nicky, who was staring off into space. "Want to see a movie?" he said, turning to look at me.

"Sure," I said. "What's playing?"

"*The Mark of Zorro* with Tyrone Power, at the Venetian."

"Your mother says he's Armenian."

"Wishful thinking. He's got black hair and he's dark-complected, so she put two and two together and made it up."

"He's handsome," I said.

"That's why she's hoping he's Armenian. Akim

Tamaroff is the only Armenian in Hollywood. He's short, fat, and has a big nose."

"He's not exactly ugly," I said.

"Not exactly, but he's no Tyrone Power."

"But the director's Armenian," I said. "Rouben Mamoulian. He's one of the best."

"I don't like his movies."

"I don't either. Should we go?"

"Yeah. Afterward we can trade baseball cards. If you want, you can stay over. Take your bike around to the back, why don't ya?" Nicky didn't ride anymore. He was two years older than me and in the ninth grade from never having flunked. The difference in our age and all didn't matter, though, because our mothers were best friends and so there was never a time when we didn't know each other.

We walked up La Salle Street to State. We might have taken the shortcut through the coal yards on Huron Street, but we didn't. We continued straight on and crossed the State Street bridge, which was my favorite bridge because the river is at its widest at this point and makes one last sweeping turn before it empties into Lake Michigan.

We leaned on the green railing and watched the boats and the sea gulls while staring down at the muddy water that was full of carp and bullheads.

Nicky didn't feel the way I did about bridges and waterways. He preferred Lake Michigan, where you could lie on the beach and go swimming. But what I liked about water was that it helped me to dream. I could follow Root River with my imagination and let it take me to all the places of the world I had never been but would someday go to. In my mind one river led to another, and even if one emptied into a lake now and then, it didn't stop there but was connected on the opposite shore with another river, and from there the journey continued. Rivers were passage-ways to the unknown. Lakes were more like cities, where one stopped and stayed. But I didn't want to stay anywhere. I wanted to go, to be on my way without any particular destination in mind. Someday I would stay, when I found my true home and place in the world, but I couldn't imag-ine when that would be, or where it would be, so I was going to be content to travel, upriver and down, until I knew who I was and what I wanted to be.

When we got to the Venetian, it was too early to go in. *The Mark of Zorro* had a half hour to go, so they weren't seating anyone.

"Should we go over to the Park Arcade?" Nicky said. "Or go across the street to Monument Square?" Nicky liked pinball games, but he didn't like pool, and it was vice versa with me.

"Let's go sit on that bench by the pool," I said. "That way we won't have to keep track of the time. We'll see the people leaving the theater when it's over." I liked sitting on the park benches with a buddy because Monument Square was the heart of downtown, and this was the city's busiest corner. Monument Square consisted of two pools and a monument. Its rectangular shape took up nearly a square block of space. I didn't know about Nicky, but I felt like a big shot sitting there and surveying the city, which I could imagine was some famous place—and not the place it actually was—and that I was famous, too, or at least interesting and important, though I couldn't think how I could be interesting and important, so all I could do was pretend to be somebody else.

"What do you want to be when you grow up?" I asked Nicky.

"A major leaguer."

"Me too," I said. "Frankie Crosetti."

"Good field, no hit."

"He can't hit the curve ball, and neither can I. But I'm working on it. Anyhow, you only get to bat like four times a game, but when you play the infield you might see the ball that many times or more in one inning. Shortstop, that's my position for life. How about you?"

"Ernie Lombardi," Nicky said. "The catcher sees the ball on every pitch. He handles the pitcher and directs the team. The only position more important is the pitcher, but I want to play every day."

Ernie Lombardi was the slowest runner in either league. He had never stolen a base and couldn't bunt. He was short and stocky, like Nicky, but he could hit the long ball—sometimes.

The movie theater was starting to empty out. From where we were sitting, we could see people streaming out the side door exit.

"No hurry," Nicky said. "It'll be a while before the comings start."

It wasn't long before the bakery next door to the Venetian was packed with people. Most of them would be buying kringle to have with their Sunday breakfasts.

For some reason I felt great inside. We were about to see a movie that was directed by an Armenian, and even if we didn't like it, there were bound to be things about it we *did* like. And besides, it was Saturday and we had almost a full day and a half before school would begin again.

PRIVATE BAKAIAN

My father shopped on Saturdays and cooked on Sundays. He had learned to cook in the Army, and after his discharge he had become a short-order cook at the Nelson Hotel. That was before he met my mother. Because after they were married, she made him leave Nelson's and go into the factory, where he could work regular hours and have the weekends off—unlike Nelson's, where he had worked the night shift and only had one day off a week, if he was lucky.

But cooking was what he was meant to do. And what he would never do again—except on Sundays. I had come to the conclusion a long time before that my dad wasn't a fighter. If he were, he would have gotten himself a restaurant or even a dinky diner somewhere, like the White Tower,

45

where he would have been his own boss and done work that was his own and that he was meant to do. I never discussed this with him. Instead, I argued about it with my mom because I felt like she was standing in his way. But she always said the same thing: He can't because he doesn't read English. . . . It's not his country. . . . He's lucky to be working and supporting a family. . . . It's what everyone else is doing. . . . We are lucky to have a roof over our heads and food on the table, et cetera.

I didn't believe her, although there were some days when I would weaken and half believe her. But even then I found it unacceptable. Because if it was true for him, then maybe it would be true for me also. Rebelling in school wasn't getting me anywhere. Maybe rebelling as an adult would produce the same result. How could I know? How could I be sure of anything?

The dining room table was set for four, but Uncle Mihran hadn't yet arrived. My mother was in the living room, the farthest room from the kitchen, embroidering one of her hankies. She was sitting at the end of the couch on the one seat where she could see into the kitchen. She was making a mistake, because if my father wanted to he could see her as well. She was his enemy on Sundays, and he was her nuisance.

It was their house, but except for Sundays she had it all to herself. She hardly made a sound when she cooked, but when he cooked the kitchen became a showplace for disorder, with everything being used at once, and effectively, although you'd never know it by appearances. Uncle Mihran said my dad was an artist—and if the results of his cooking were the proof, then there was no doubt that Uncle Mihran was right. My mother was pleased with the food but not by his other artistic results.

His one mistake was asking my mother where things were kept. He never could find anything when he needed it, and when he needed something he needed it *now*. If she could have produced what he wanted without a sound, it might have been okay, but she couldn't do that. She had only to utter a single comment—as she always did—and he would commence to roar like a wounded lion, pick up a knife, and chase her around the kitchen table and out of the room. He of course didn't hear a word she said.

But I did! And I tried to see it from both her side and his. I wasn't in agreement with either of them. I would scream for peace because peace was all that *I* wanted. I simply couldn't understand that he didn't mean anything by chasing her with a knife. I thought he meant it. I thought he meant to kill her. And that it was only a matter of time before he would.

Whenever I entered the house on Sunday afternoons—and I made it a point to stay away for as long as I could—I'd check the walls to see if they had been sprayed with blood. By now I knew better, but that didn't help how I felt about their fights, and my worries over my mother's safety.

I had learned from an incident that had happened early in the summer that my father did not intend to actually harm my mother, only to threaten her. It was natural, I learned, that he would do it with a knife. It had to do with his background. I had come to this conclusion during the *Madagh*, our annual church picnic, when I saw my father performing a solo dance with a knife clenched tightly between his teeth. I was scared at first, if not terrified, but somehow with the music playing, the people clapping and chanting, it seemed in some odd way to be natural—that is, natural for an Armenian. And some part of me could see that it was not really crazy at all.

I tried to think what it all meant, and I finally came to the conclusion that knives were the common weapons used by the Armenians in the Old Country, since they were not allowed to bear arms in Turkey. For that reason probably everyone carried a knife. I remembered that in photos I had seen they carried their knives in their cummerbunds, so they would be handy in an emergency. Isn't that what the cowboys did in the movies—reach for their guns whenever anything was in doubt? And if they didn't reach for them, they fingered them slyly or looked down at them tucked neatly in their holsters, ready for action.

I wasn't sure if my mom and dad had already had their fight when I walked into the house, but at least there wasn't any blood on the kitchen walls. I knew better than to check, but I couldn't help myself. I peered into the kitchen and nonchalantly looked things over. My father, at that moment, wasn't even cooking. He was staring out the kitchen window while puffing on a cigarette. When he saw me, he walked into the dining room and sat down. "Everything rest now," he said in English. "Maybe I'm resting it now, too."

I was glad to see he was in a good mood. "Chicken?" I said, because that's what he usually cooked on Sundays. He nodded, pleased with himself and his afternoon of work. "Tell me about the first time you cooked chicken," I said. It was an old story, but I never tired of hearing it.

"Not first time, first time officers' mess." This was an American story, and he was using English to tell it.

"I was cooking in the kitchen full-time," he began, creating the setting in our language. "We were cooking chicken. For the troops we'd cut the chickens up into parts, but for the officers we had to serve the chicken whole. That wasn't my job. That was the job of the head cook, who made it special, cooking the officers' chickens himself, adding this and that, and then serving them on a special platter, carving them at the table, and so on. But the head cook was hung over. He couldn't cook. He was still in the sack. So they told me, 'Bedros, you cook the officers' chicken today.'"

"So you served the chicken that day?" I said.

"That's right. I cook chicken, I serve chicken, and so on."

"What happened next?" I asked, trying to keep a straight face.

"Time passes, yes. We're cleaning up. The Lieutenant walks into kitchen and says it to me, 'Bedros, the Captain wants to see you.'

"What's I do wrong? I thinks me. If Captain mad, bring trouble, yes. I quick remove apron, roll down sleeves, and so on. I follow Lieutenant into officers' mess. I come up to Captain's table." At this point my father stopped speaking and got to his feet, placing his cigarette in the ashtray.

He clicked his heels and stood at rigid attention. Then he saluted and spoke. "Private Bakaian reporting, sir."

"Private Bakaian," the Captain answers. But I cannot be sure from my father's voice what the Captain is feeling. Is he puzzled, is he amused, is he curious? Who is this Private Bakaian? Maybe there is a question in his voice.

"Yes, sir," my father answers, nervous now but beginning to swell with pride because he knows what is coming next.

"Very good chicken I eat today, Private Bakaian. I ask, who cook this chicken? They tell me Private Bakaian, he cook it. Is that so?"

"Yes, sir," my father says once again, his eyes staring straight ahead, the color rising in his face.

"I want start you tomorrow cook officers' mess. Be my cook from now on."

"Yes, sir!" my father says for the last time, and once again he salutes and clicks his heels. But this

50

time he is unable to turn around as he had done then, so very long ago. His chair is directly behind him, so he sits down. He smiles to himself, picks up his cigarette from the ashtray, and flicks the ash, his face flushed and happy.

It was a thrilling story, and I never tired of hearing it. It was my father's one moment of triumph in a life of frustration. At least that's how I saw it. But it was more than that for me. It was much, much more for me than that. What it told me was that if they know you are good, you will be rewarded. Ability is what counts. If you're good at something, if you're the best, then that's it, you can do what you want. No one will stop you.

But I wasn't sure I believed it. Yet I wanted to believe it. I wanted so badly to believe that it was true that I *did* believe it—almost!

THE ARMENIAN FENCE

Another horrible year of school had come to an end. But this time I made it. I passed the fifth grade at last, which meant that I had only one year left at Garfield.

It was summer again, my favorite season of the year. The garden had been dug, and my dad was getting ready to put his seeds in the ground. But first he decided it was time we painted our fence. "What color you think it we paint fence?" he asked me one morning over breakfast. I was naturally suspicious because he had just spoken in English.

"Do you want my help?" I asked without committing myself.

"Of course," my mother said. "Father and son, you can do it together."

"Blue," I said.

"Naturally," my mother said, "your favorite color."

My father looked from my mother to me without speaking. "Is that the right color for a fence?" he said. "Let us consider for a moment. Blue! The sky is blue. Every day we see the sky. Every day we look at something blue. Should we have a fence also colored blue? What color blue did you have in mind?"

"Light blue," I said.

"That's his favorite color," my mother said without turning from the stove.

My father dunked his *choreg* in his coffee and thought to himself. "Maybe," he said at last, "you shouldn't waste your favorite color on a fence."

"He doesn't think blue is appropriate," my mother said to me, as if the discussion only involved the two of us.

"What color did you have in mind?" I asked my dad. He pronounced an Armenian word that wasn't in my vocabulary. "I haven't the English word," I said.

"It is between yellow and brown," my mother said.

"You mean ocher," I said. "That's a pretty strange color for a fence—or for anything else. In this country, at least."

My father dunked his *choreg* in his coffee and didn't speak. I dunked mine in my tea. We were staring at each other across the table. He finished his *choreg* and downed the rest of his coffee. I didn't say anything. After a couple of minutes he pushed his chair away from the table and stood up. He was still in his BVD's, and barefoot, as usual.

After he had walked into the bedroom to get dressed, my mother turned from the stove and spoke to me in a whisper. "It reminds him of the Old Country. Try not to make a fight."

"I'm not looking to make a fight, but ocher's an ugly color. I mean, *nobody* has *ever* painted a fence ocher. It's unheard of. Can't we find something else to remind him of the Old Country?"

"Don't be impossible. He wants your help. And he wants an Armenian color for the fence. The garden reminds him of Armenia, the dirt reminds him of his village, the vegetables he grows remind him of his home in Kharpet. That's why he's so angry. He's tormented by remembering, and he feels tormented when he forgets. Let him have his way."

At the hardware store I asked the clerk to show us the paint chart. I went down the chart till I found ocher. I showed the color swatch to my dad. "What do you think?"

"It needs a little brown, and a touch of red."

"I don't think they mix that way," I said.

"Why not?"

"It's not a standard color. They can't guarantee the result."

"I'll guarantee it. Two drops of brown, one drop of red. Two gallons. I don't need to see it—just have him mix it."

I told the clerk what my dad had said. He looked us up and down, smiled weakly, and disappeared into the back room.

"No problem," I said to my dad.

"You will see," my father said. "We have picked the right color for a fence."

ARMENIAN SCHOOL

I could no longer get out of attending Armenian School classes. They were held Wednesday evenings in the cellar of the Armenian church on State Street.

My mother hadn't pressured me to attend before now because she knew I didn't want to go. But it must have been hard for her to make excuses for me, since she was one of the two regular teachers.

The church cellar, whose entrance was on Wilson Street, consisted of a hallway, with a kitchen and bathroom on either side, opening out into an auditorium-sized room with a raised platform for plays, speeches, recitations, and the like. Inside this space, along the wall facing Wilson Street, were two rooms that were used for a variety of purposes:

cloak and storage rooms, kindergarten classes, et cetera. On Wednesday evenings these were quickly converted into classrooms for beginning and advanced pupils. What was being taught was the language itself; that is, reading and writing. For although everyone spoke Armenian at home, nearly everyone was illiterate, not only the children, but their parents as well.

My mother had presented me with the book I would be using before she went off to class ahead of me. I had sat down on my bed and looked it over. There were drawings ornamenting each of the letters, with additional drawings throughout the book. It wasn't so different from the books I remembered in the first grade except that the people being drawn were Armenians, not Americans, and the scenes that were depicted were of another country. I wondered if the country was Armenia, since I had never before seen pictures of my parents' homeland, except for a few snapshots.

It was obvious that our grammar book had not been produced in America. Everything about it, from the binding to the paper to the drawings and printing, seemed Old Country, which was only another word in my vocabulary for "backward."

At the same time it had a feeling of familiarity, but of what I wasn't sure. After all, I had spoken only Armenian until my mother sent me to nursery school at age four, which meant that Armenian was my mother tongue.

When I got to the church, the class of older students had just let out. They were milling about, waiting for the next class to begin.

"Look who's here," Hatch Kevorkian said when I walked into the room, "*Deegen* Zabel's boy. So you finally broke down."

I shrugged my shoulders and looked around the room. If I was going to be razzed, then no matter what I said it would only be used against me.

"Don't pay him any attention," Rose Parsegian, one of the older girls, said to me.

"I'm not," I said. "It's a free country. He can say whatever he likes."

"You're not too good for us, are you?" Peter Baleozian said.

"Maybe I'm not good enough for you," I said. "Isn't that what you really mean?"

"I don't know," Pete said. "I only know you never come around for church services, you don't belong to any of the clubs, you never act in the plays. . . ."

"What is he, on trial?" Rose said. "He hasn't been here two minutes, and already you're on his back."

"That's okay," I said. "I can take it. Pete's entitled to his opinion, small as it is. What I do with my free time is my business. If some people want to go from home to church and back again, they've got that right. And I've got the right not to."

Rose didn't agree with me, so she shut up. Probably no one agreed with me.

My mother clapped her hands to indicate that it was time for classes to resume. I didn't like the expression on her face. I could tell that she had been listening to our conversation. She took the older class, and Mrs. Avakian took our class of beginners.

I felt like I was in the first grade again. Except this time the lessons were easy. We opened our books to the first page. "*Aye, pen, keem*," Mrs. Avakian said, and paused before repeating with her thick accent, "A, B, C." She then recited the thirty-six letters of our alphabet.

Mrs. Avakian went from the recitation of the alphabet to different drills to help us memorize the letters. Before long we were writing out the letters and practicing our penmanship, which was one of the few things I had enjoyed in regular school. I felt comfortable with the other kids and not the least bit threatened. But I also felt stifled, being in such a small room. I didn't like the smell of the cellar any more than I liked the smell of the church floor above. It made me feel sad.

I got home before my mother did. I was sitting in the living room reading when she walked in the door. I watched her remove her hat and hang up her coat. She went into the kitchen to speak to my dad before walking back through the dining room and then into the living room, where she took a seat across from me.

She was waiting for me to tell her about the class, but she could see that I didn't want to discuss it. "You're not like the others," she said.

"I know."

"Why aren't you like the others?"

"I wish I knew, but I don't."

"What is it that's bothering you?"

"You wouldn't understand."

"If I don't know what's bothering you, I can't possibly understand, can I?"

"I don't want to be a sad Armenian. I don't like being looked down on. I feel backward and unwanted, and it's worse when I'm with the Armenians."

"They embarrass you."

"Yes."

"You know how your face looks when you're in church?"

"No," I said. "I have no idea."

"Frightened. You don't look out of place, but you do look frightened. What is that about?"

I had to think. I was also trying to decide what to tell her and what not to tell her. I didn't like the look of worried concern on her face. It made me feel bad. My mother always listened to me and encouraged me, and I knew she believed in me, even if I did drive her crazy most of the time. I owed her an explanation. "I guess my biggest fear is that I'm going to starve to death. That I'm going to be abandoned, lying in the streets, with nowhere to turn, and that I'm slowly going to starve."

"*Yavroos*, we came to this country so we *wouldn't* starve. That will never happen here."

"I don't think about it all the time. It just pops into my head sometimes."

"Is that your big fear?"

"No. I don't have any big fears, unless it's that I'm going to be stuck here when it's time for me to leave, and when that happens I'll end up working in a factory and never get to know the world and all the people living in it."

"I didn't know you felt that way."

"I'm not sure I know what I mean. I'm not even sure I know what I want. I just know what I *don't* want."

"You're saying that you don't belong here."

"I won't always be here is what I mean. I don't know if there is any place where I belong, but I believe there will be such a place, depending on what I do with my life. I just know whatever it is I need to happen, it can never happen here."

"Thirteen years old, and already such big thoughts."

"What kind of thoughts did you have at thirteen?"

"Much different. I was very old at thirteen. I missed my childhood. I never completed my childhood. With one part of me I wanted to go back. With another part I did what had to be done. I was *jarbeek*. I always took the next step."

"You were a survivor."

My mother looked at me for a long minute. "I am a part of two worlds, one lost and shattered, the other a compromise. Now you tell me it is the same with you."

"It's not your fault," I said. "It's just the way it is."

"I don't want you to be lonely."

"That's not one of my fears," I said. "I've always been lonely."

BOOK TWO

BASEBALL CARDS

Of the two hundred Armenian families in Racine the most interesting by far—in my opinion—was the Tekeyans. Nicky's father was one of the few Armenian men who didn't work in a factory. He owned a restaurant-bar on Douglas Avenue that he ran with his brother. Compared to us, they were rich, which was why Arpey could buy as many records and movie magazines as she liked and why Nicky could play the pinball games. But it wasn't money that made them interesting—it was something else. They had style and intelligence. And also they were very eccentric. On top of that they were miserable—but each in his own way, so that when they were all together they really made a scene. It was better than going to a movie or a play. A feeling of excitement came over me whenever I was in their home, because without even trying they were teaching me about books, movies, jazz, art, and all kinds of other things that most people I knew didn't ever think about.

But although they were inspiring to me, they weren't inspiring to themselves. Nicky's father, Krikor, was always hollering at Nicky's mom because she never stayed home, and she was mad at him for throwing his money around. The children were angry with their mom because she seldom cooked or cleaned house, and they were mad at their father for the same reason their mother was—and also because he was never home, either.

But why Nicky and his brother and sisters were unhappy with themselves was harder to figure out. Avak was angry because of what the Armenians had been through, which they were always reminding him of, which he said was interfering with his life. And so he didn't know where he was going or what to do with himself. Eva felt unloved, and Arpey was sick all the time. (The Armenians said her mother tried to abort her and the medicines she took while she was pregnant had permanently damaged her.) Lily didn't have the privacy she needed, and although she was supposed to be going off to Juilliard, so far she hadn't left home. Avak was in his last year of high school, and the girls had all graduated. Nicky wasn't miserable—he was just sad, but he was trying to fight his way out of it.

The funny thing, I guess, was that they never affected me the way they affected themselves. Like I said, they were the most exciting Armenian family in town.

Sunday was the saddest day of the week. The city was dead. Everyone was locked up in their homes. The church bells rang mournfully, the people dressed unnaturally, and everything seemed to be out of kilter. Also, except in summer, it was the last day of freedom before school began again for another week. The only good thing about Sunday was that it was the best day to visit Nicky and his family because all of them were likely to be home.

My mom and dad always went to church on Sundays. I liked being alone in the mornings because that was the best time to draw and write in my diary. But I wanted to leave the house before they got back and before my father began cooking the Sunday dinner.

I carried my bike onto Nicky's porch and leaned it against the rails. There was a discussion going on in the living room, and on the record player in the dining room there was an Armenian record playing. It was Shah-Mouradian, Nicky's father's favorite, singing one of those Old Country songs that's so sad it makes you wish you were dead. I followed Nicky into his bedroom, where the ball game was on—Yankees versus the White Sox—which is how I knew for sure he'd be home. "It's a lucky thing we saved our baseball cards," Nicky said, closing the door.

"Yeah," I said, and waited for him to tell me why.

"Now we can try to perfect our card collections. Have a look at the back of this comic. It lists all the ones produced so far. A perfect collection consists of two hundred twenty-five."

"How many do you have?"

"Over one hundred fifty."

"That's way more than me. I'll never make it."

"Want to trade your cards for something else, like one of my board games? Or some movie magazines?"

"Those are all Arpey's."

"She'll never know. I'll help you steal them."

"Nah," I said. "I think I'll hang on to the cards I've got. I like going over them."

"Think DiMaggio will break the consecutive game hitting record?" Nicky said.

"He only needs three more games."

"Two. He got a hit in the first inning. Let's bet something on how far he'll go. What's your guess?"

"No fair," I said. "The guy that goes first doesn't stand a chance. If I say forty, you'll say forty-one, so then anything higher than forty you automatically win."

"But if it's under forty, you win."

"Yeah, but it's nearly that now."

"Then guess fifty."

"Oh, yeah, I know you. You'll guess forty-nine."

"He could top fifty," Nicky said.

"Fat chance," I said. "Even DiMaggio couldn't get a hit in fifty straight games."

"Let's go have some lemonade and a Spam sandwich," Nicky said. "Lily just brought home some fresh *peda*."

All the time we had been talking, I was watching Avak through the cracked door. The discussion in the living room had turned into a shouting match. Avak was biting down hard on his index finger, which was his way of restraining himself from committing violence. I was watching in amazement, and suddenly I saw that he had two strangers living inside himself that were of equal strength—one invisible (the good guy) who was causing him to revolt, and the other (the bad guy) who was doing the revolting. His face had slowly turned red, and now his neck was bulging out. He was stomping across the room while alternately cursing and biting his finger, which had become as white and swollen as his rage. "Avak's pacing again in the other room," I said to Nicky in answer.

"Don't pay any attention. Just follow me into the kitchen."

"He never hollers at me," I said.

"That's not the point. Just don't look at him, so he doesn't think he has an audience."

"Got ya," I said. "I'll sneak in behind you."

Nicky walked toward the kitchen through the living room, but when he passed Avak, who was ranting away, he gave him a sidearm punch with the back of his clenched fist. Avak wheeled around and landed a punch on Nicky's forearm and gave out a roar of pleasure. Nicky crouched into his boxer's stance—he had been secretly working out in the YMCA gym, hoping to compete in the Golden Gloves—and threw two quick punches into Avak's midriff. Avak parried with two well-aimed body shots of his own, cursing with pleasure, while Nicky smiled wolfishly to himself. Avak burst out laughing. "C'mon, fatso," he bellowed, "put 'em up." He was still grinding away on his index finger. He threw a series of staccato punches with his left, while shouting, "Who do you think you are to challenge your big brother? Ha! Haven't you any respect? I'll destroy you. I'll turn you into mincemeat for *kufta*, you sheepherder, you Armenian cucumber."

Nicky faked a shot to the stomach, faked a shot to the head, and landed a one-two punch, left, right, to Avak's forearm—and declared himself the winner by strutting away, as if his brother had just been liquidated. Avak ran beside him, wheeled around, and gave him a swift kick in the rear with the back of his foot that sent Nicky stumbling into the kitchen. I followed quickly behind and got between them and, sticking two fingers in my mouth, I whistled the fight to a close.

MR. HUBER

It was the first day of school. Sixth grade. One more year, and I'd be on my way to Washington Junior—and whatever lay beyond.

But I had gotten off on the wrong foot again. We weren't in the room fifteen minutes when I got sent out to the hall. Our teacher, Miss Simpson, wanted to seat us alphabetically, which put me in the front seat, one row over from the window.

"I want to sit by the window," I said, "and I don't want to sit in the front seat." I hadn't bothered to raise my hand to ask permission to speak.

"Well!" she exclaimed. "I see you haven't learned anything about conduct after five grades in our school, but I will see to it that you learn how to behave in my class, or else. Just go sit in the hall, young man, until I decide to have you in my room."

I was so mad I could have spit. I didn't see why I should be punished for speaking my mind. Even if everyone else kept their mouths shut tight, it didn't make keeping my mouth shut the right thing to do. I was old enough to have rights.

The janitor walked by and shook his head at me, as if I were some kind of hopeless case. I followed him with my eyes and scowled. He didn't scare me.

All kinds of thoughts were going through my head, none of them worth repeating out loud. All at once I remembered that we were supposed to get a new principal. When I first heard the rumor, I had hoped it was true, because whoever came along would have to be an improvement over the principal we had—old man Snyder, who had never learned any of our names or taken the least interest in our activities, especially our school-yard activities, like sports.

At that moment I looked up to see a tall man in a pin-striped suit, with bow tie, come marching down the hall. He glanced at me as he hurried by. I still had the scowl on my face that I had put on for the janitor.

To my surprise he turned around—after he had walked out of my sight—and came back and stood facing me.

I didn't bother to change my expression. He said, "How would you like to catch some fungoes?"

I was almost too startled to speak. But I didn't hesitate for long, even though I only half believed he was telling the truth. When we got to his office, I was surprised to see a bat and ball in the corner by his desk.

Without saying a word to his secretary, he grabbed up his equipment—which included a mitt for me—and we started down the steps to the school yard.

"Tell me your name," he said, as we walked out the door. "Mine's Max Huber."

"Sure, Mr. Huber," I said, "but it's kind of complicated. I'm Stepan to my parents, and Steven to my teachers and some of the others, but my friends call me Step."

"Okay, Step," Mr. Huber said. "What would you like, grounders or fly balls?"

"Grounders," I said. "I'm an infielder."

Mr. Huber was holding the bat over his shoulder with his left hand while tossing the ball up and catching it with his right. "You're not in position," he said.

"Oh!" I answered, and realized that he was right. I crouched and slammed my fist into the glove, improving the pocket. My heart was thumping so loudly it frightened me.

He hit a weak grounder in front of me. I came charging in and took it bare-handed and looped it back to him.

"Good play," he called out. "I think you had him at first."

"Home plate, too," I said, "if there had been a runner on third trying to score." I slammed my glove again, making it pop.

He hit the next several grounders really hard, and I made clean pickups each time. I was so charged up I didn't think I'd ever make an error on any ball I could put a glove on.

The next grounders he hit were to my left. Some were easy pickups, and others I had to work hard to reach. I still hadn't let one get by me.

"You're doing good," Mr. Huber said, but this time he hit one to my right. I knocked it down back-handed and picked it up at once. "I would have had him at first," I shouted.

He hit another to my right, but this time I flubbed it. "You don't go to your right as well as to your left," Mr. Huber shouted.

"No one does."

"That's no reason for you not to," he shouted back, and hit a fiery grounder that nearly went through my legs. "Do you know why?"

"It's hard to turn the glove in reverse and still have control over the pocket," I said.

"That's half of it," Mr. Huber said. "You're in such a hurry to go to your right that you take your eye off the ball. That's not true when you go to your left, if you've noticed."

"I think you're right," I said. "Thanks."

"We'll work on it sometime," Mr. Huber said. "My secretary's been at the window for ten minutes now, trying to get my attention. We'd better go back inside."

I kept pounding the glove as we walked to the front door and up the stairs, and I nearly forgot to give it back when we got to his office. "Here," I said, "and thanks a lot for the game."

Mr. Huber turned and smiled at me. "Keep your eye on the ball," he said, and disappeared inside his office.

I took my seat outside the door of my classroom. I was glad to be alone, and I no longer felt embarrassed. All kinds of thoughts were flying around in my head. I was sure I had learned something big, but I couldn't say that I knew what it was. Mr. Huber had made me feel important, and that was enough in itself, because I realized that I had never felt that way in all the years I had been at Garfield.

SCOUT'S WOODS

October has always been my favorite month. The autumn leaves turn color, and when they do, everything seems to grow quiet and there is a feeling that the elements of nature are beginning to return to where they belong.

The place I liked to go when I wanted to be alone was Scout's Woods, which began at the edge of town where State Street turned into Highway 38. To get there, you had to cross two open fields that were divided by a row of abandoned apple trees. From there the land sloped abruptly into a wooded area. On the side of the hill that ran down to the river was a natural spring where I always stopped to have a drink. At the bottom of the slope there was a marshy area caused by the continual flow of water from the spring. I sometimes walked across the log that had fallen over the marsh, or else took the long walk around. It was a popular spot for game animals and birds, with woodcock favoring the slope below the spring, ducks preferring the marsh, and rabbits and pheasants the field just beyond that bordered the river. I'd never walked from the spring to the river without flushing game, and it was always a shock and a thrill when it happened.

But my destination, if I had one, was the swinging bridge that skirted the wild fields at the edge of the golf course. At that time of year there were never more than one or two pairs of golfers on the course, and their dress and movements seemed to blend with the flow of the land and nature's changing colors. And they were friendly in a way that they never were in the summer, when they made me feel that I was intruding on their sacred property.

I liked to wear my parka when I went tramping, not only for the warmth but also because it seemed the right garment to wear in the outdoors. I also liked to wear it because it had two big pockets, one for the sandwich that I always made myself and wrapped in wax paper, and the other for my notebook—because I always wrote and sketched when I went by myself to Scout's Woods. When I reached the middle of the bridge, I sat down with my legs dangling over the side, facing upstream, away from the golf course. I looked down at the water and let its stillness enter me, feeling inspired by the sense of oneness in things, because it seemed at that moment that I was a part of everything that was. I opened my notebook and started to write.

Why does the river turn black at this season of the year and seem to slow and grow quiet and wait? Is it returning to its source or settling into itself—as the leaves settle to the ground around the tree that bore them, where they will rest and wait until they rise and turn again into leaves, as you must settle, gentle river, into this season of dying, until you flow again at the passing of winter, at the coming of spring. . . .

I didn't hear the golfers approaching until their footsteps rattled the bridge. One of them said, "You've got a good day for it, son."

I closed my notebook. "Sure," I said. "I guess you do, too."

"Every warm day is a gift from now on," the other golfer said.

"You've got the course to yourself," I said.

"So have you," the first one said.

"I know," I said. "That's the way I like it."

They both laughed good-naturedly. And then they were gone. I stuck my notebook in my pocket and crossed the bridge onto the golf course. I thought I'd go sit on a bunker and eat my sandwich and see what the gophers were up to. Maybe I'd make a sketch of one of them, or else just draw the trees.

THE BRIDGE AND THE PARK

It was November, the saddest time of the year, being neither autumn nor winter. I decided to take a walk to the park that was just three blocks from our house. It overlooked Main Street, with a view of Lake Michigan in the distance. It was a small triangular park perched on a knoll, and its lone bench was almost always vacant during the late afternoon on Fridays because everyone was cashing their checks and shopping or getting spruced up for the evening. It meant I could be alone with my thoughts, undisturbed, and with a chance to look out on the city without being noticed by anyone.

When I got to the park, two dogs were chasing each other through the bushes that bordered the lower corner, near the fountain. I moved the lone bench to give myself the view I wanted and sat down.

The State Street bridge in the distance had just opened, and the boat it had let through seemed to grow in size as it headed in my direction. It must have been carrying food because it was being shadowed by sea gulls. I followed the river with my eyes, from the State Street bridge to the Main Street bridge, which lay directly beneath my view.

Beyond the river, the cars moved swiftly in opposite directions, with more of them heading toward the downtown than away from it. I followed their movement until my sight was blocked by the building at the corner of Main and State, where I was able to make out the roof of the Main Street Theatre, and also the facade of the bowling alley that had once been the Rex Theatre during the days of silent movies.

I began to wonder, as I had so often, why it seemed that everything was more possible at such moments. I looked down at the river and dreamed its meaning. It seemed so different from ours. Whenever I dreamed the river I dreamed myself, not as I was, with all my problems, but as someone free, yet still connected to everything. I wished I could move with the freedom of water, and also like the birds that moved above the water. How easy it seemed for them, and for the river, to just be and do, without any thought as to how or why. So why was it so hard for us? I wondered.

It didn't seem to me that life should be as difficult as it was. And I couldn't understand why my thoughts and feelings should remain as they were, confused and without direction. Why couldn't I make a change in myself by making something outside of myself, like the man who had made the rock garden? Every time I viewed his work, I felt a mysterious change come over me. It instilled in me the same sense of wonder that I felt in front of nature. Was there a word for such work? And if there was, who could tell me the word?

Instead of going home, I headed up Erie Street to Hamilton and then turned onto La Salle Street until I got to Nicky's home. It was just getting dark, and I was afraid no one was home because the lights in the living room and dining room weren't on. Only the kitchen light was burning at the back of the house. When I closed the front door behind me, *Deegen* Roxie appeared in the kitchen door. "Hello, Stepan," she said. "Have you eaten? I'm making *zhkmela monte*."

"No thanks, *Deegen* Roxie," I said. "We ate at five o'clock, as usual. My dad's always starving when he gets home from the factory. Is Nicky here?"

"They've all gone shopping. All but Lily. But they should be home soon, if they don't go to the movies. Do you want to play a record and wait? You love *zhkmela monte*."

"Not as much as Avak," I said.

She laughed and rubbed her hands across her apron before disappearing into the kitchen.

I didn't want to play a record by myself, but I didn't want to go home, either. I could always wait in Nicky's room, I thought to myself as I began climbing the stairs.

The light was shining beneath Lily's closed door. I hesitated and then I knocked.

"Come in, Stepan."

"How did you know it was me?" I said as I closed the door behind me.

"By your walk."

"You did?"

"Why don't you sit down?"

"I was over at Colbert Park," I said, "and then I came here. Friday nights are sure busy."

"You don't like to shop?"

"I don't like crowds."

"I have the same problem." Lily smiled to show that we were in cahoots.

I smiled back, feeling relaxed. "Do you ever think it's funny that everything in nature seems natural and right and that it isn't something we have to try and understand, whereas whenever man makes something or does something, he puts a label on it if it's something familiar . . . or else . . . well, now I'm confused."

"Were you thinking of something specific?"

"Well, actually I was. The rock garden by Island Park next to the Liberty Street bridge. Does that kind of thing have a name? Well, not a name exactly, a definition, I guess I mean?"

"A number of names," Lily said, and smiled, seeming pleased by what I said.

"It's not what they do that interests me, but *why* they do it. Because that might explain the effect it has on me."

"They are imitating nature, I suppose."

"Why?"

"Because nature is complete, it's actual, it's already realized. And we aren't, or haven't been."

"Haven't been what?"

"Realized—actualized—completed."

"We haven't?"

"You're funny," Lily said, smiling again. "But seriously, I'm glad you *know* that you're troubled about this, because *everyone* is, but not everyone knows it. That's why people drink, get divorced, have fights, and go to war. These are people who haven't heard the question—inside themselves, I mean. Then there are those who have—more or less—and they get married, hold down jobs, have families, and so on. You're almost too young to ask the question, but I'm glad you have. Just don't be in too big a hurry to find the answer."

"I don't think anyone knows what life is for," I said.

"Wait a minute. Don't talk so fast—and don't talk so big. What you mean is, *you* don't understand what life is for."

I blushed. She was right. She had found what was troubling me and had given me my question. "How can I know?" I asked.

"By what you do. By what is natural for you. We are part of nature, after all, which means that we *can* know things—certainly those things that come naturally to us. Name some of the things that interest you. Things that you do."

"I like to make lists," I said, which was the first thing that popped into my head.

"Order," Lily said. "What else?"

"I like to draw."

"Form," she said. "And when you were younger, you used to like to color in books, and you were better at it than anyone else. Remember?"

"And what is that?" I asked.

"Proportion, color sense, aesthetics."

"I keep a diary," I said. "It's not just about what I've done that day, but thoughts I've had, descriptions of things I like and want to remember. Stuff like that."

"Understanding," Lily said, "and that's where your question came from—from wanting to understand more about life."

"So where does that leave me?"

Lily's smile turned into a laugh this time. "Just where you've always been—but a lot closer to understanding just *where* that is. Be yourself! Don't agree, just to get along; don't disagree, just to be different. Sometimes it's best to speak up; sometimes it's best to keep silent. Do you still run away from home?"

"No," I said, "but I still think about it. How did you know?"

"I saw you once, late at night, at the paperback rack at Ace Grill. I had come out of the Rialto Theater after the last show, and I saw you as I walked by. The streets were all deserted, and there were only two people at the counter—single men drinking coffee. Somehow I knew you'd be going home before long."

"I always went home," I said, "sooner or later. I used to think running away was from being mad at my parents, but I realize now, for the first time, that it's because I'm confused about myself—and angry because of it."

"Are they still giving you a hard time at school?"

"Not so much, not anymore, but I'll never get back those two years they flunked me."

"Don't be so sure."

I felt puzzled again. What did her statement mean? Just then the front door opened and closed. "It's Nicky," Lily said. "He just walked in. Shall we join him?"

UNCLE MIHRAN

"Must you rebel against everything?" my mother shouted. Unlike my father, she rarely lost her temper with me. But I had just put my foot down, telling her I would no longer attend Armenian language classes at the church.

"What good is it?" I asked. "When would I ever use it? Who knows the Armenian language but the Armenians, anyway? We don't even have a country anymore. The Russians own us now, and who cares about them, even, much less us."

"That's not why you're not going," she said. "It's because you're ashamed and embarrassed. You think you're too good."

She was right, but I didn't want to admit it. I avoided looking at my father, who was already furious with me, but couldn't think of anything to say that my mother hadn't already said. I looked instead at Uncle Mihran, who was sitting on the opposite end of the sofa from my dad. He looked from me to my mother before speaking. "Let him be," he said. "We think it is hard only for us, but it is also hard for them. Our understanding is imperfect. He has Armenian thoughts that are not his, and are therefore incomprehensible to him, and he has American thoughts that he can't direct because he doesn't know where they come from, either. Let him be confused. What is the harm in that? You can't force him, and if you try it will only make matters worse."

"Let it be worse," my father said. "In that way it can only get better. He will understand when he is grown. Until then he can listen to us."

"Don't talk about me that way," I screamed. "I'm not a dog to be put on a leash."

"He is like you," my mother said to Uncle Mihran, "headstrong, rebellious. Ever since the Armenian church split in two, you have refused both sides."

"I go to the Presbyterian church," Uncle Mihran said. "There is only one God. In our church God is judged by our fortunes. Since our Massacre at the hands of the Turks he's lost his popularity. After the Massacres politics entered the church, then more grievances, and finally murder. In the church! The Archbishop! Those crazy Tashnaks. The *odars* almost cannot believe what we have done. I almost cannot believe what we have done. I will not forget by going to the *odar* church, but at least the reminder is missing."

I knew what my uncle was talking about. The Tashnaks were a radical political party who insisted on having the flag of the defunct Armenian nation displayed in the church. But Armenia was now a part of Russia, and Etchmiadzin, our Holy See, was also under the sovereignty of Russia. The Tashnaks had murdered the Archbishop in New York, during the church service, for refusing to mount the Armenian flag.

"Let's not discuss it," my father was saying. "What is done cannot be undone. Once the arrow has left the bow, it cannot be called back."

"We cannot fight the Turk, so we fight one another," Uncle Mihran said. "The Turk hates us, and we have come to hate ourselves, and only because their hatred worked, it was effective. What they couldn't kill off they expelled, and now we are like an angry cloud blown across the face of the land. Strangers take us in, but among ourselves we argue and fight."

"What you say is true and not true," my mother said. "We have banded together here, and a new generation has been born. Take a wife and have a child. You will see—there is hope. It is in our children's eyes."

"But from your children's eyes a different world is seen than the one you look at," Uncle Mihran answered. "If they are your hope, what is their hope, hah? Can you know it? Can *they* know it? *Will* they know it if they follow in your footsteps and not their own, hah?"

"What are their footsteps? Show me their footsteps," my father commanded.

I watched as the adults stared at one another in silence. Finally, Uncle Mihran spoke. "Stepan, would you like to come to my church on the corner next Sunday?"

"Sure," I said. "Why not?"

THE BLACK STOCKINGS

"**W**hat do you want?" It was my mother again, after me, wanting something—not just for me, but for herself. "Listen to me. Have I told you the story of the black stockings?"

"You've tried," I said. We had been over this so many times before—and I knew without knowing that her story was something more than I could bear. I knew she had suffered, that she had nearly lost her leg and bore a hideous scar from a bomb that had killed two of her relatives and had nearly crippled her. I also knew that she had been orphaned. That we had no relatives, no family photos, no relics from the past. But why would I want to hear about such things? They had happened so long ago, in a place I couldn't even visualize, and concerned an enemy I had never met or even seen, for there were no Turkish families in our town. "I'm not going to listen to you," I said.

"This is not a terrible story. It's not going to hurt you. It hurt me once, a long time ago, but I'm glad it happened because it proved something—to me! When I was a young girl, not much older than you are now, I fell in love with a young man in Piraeus, in Greece, where I later met your father's family. He played a mandolin. We took walks together. We even went to a movie once after we were engaged. Did you know that? His name was Dickran.

"When it came time for the marriage, my future mother-in-law took me shopping and bought me black stockings because she was in mourning for her husband, who had been murdered by the Turks in Smyrna, where they had always lived. Well, I refused to wear those black stockings, and I backed out of the marriage. You see, she had put her unhappiness ahead of my happiness. Even on my wedding day I was going to be deprived, and not only deprived, but humiliated. That's how it felt to me then. I said no. You see, I had my own mind, I was independent in my thinking, and so that comes from me, how you are. But I was not stubborn, I was not naughty. I knew what I wanted. And I went after it! So what do *you* want?"

"I want to be free."

"Tsk!" she exclaimed, pressing her tongue against the roof of her mouth. "That's what I wanted. So I came to America. Would I want something for myself and not want the same for you? This is a free country, isn't it? You are free, aren't you? What kind of talk is this?"

"Safety and freedom are two different things. Your earned your safety, I suppose, and I guess I was born into safety—but freedom is something else. And it's different for everyone. Every time I am stopped, it is because I am not free. And everything seems to want to stop me."

"For instance?"

I looked her in the eye, considering what to say, and how to say it. I wanted to say, "Being born," just to silence her, because that was how I felt sometimes.

She was waiting for an answer. "Flunking," I said. "Being flunked because I'm Armenian and don't give a damn about what they have to teach about their great civilization. It'll be great if I'm a part of it. Otherwise the world can blow itself to hell."

"You flunked because you didn't pay attention. Now you have good grades, there will be no more flunking. Your conduct is still bad, but it is also improving. They can't fail you anymore."

"It has nothing to do with conduct or paying attention. They made us change our names, way back in the early grades. That's where the trouble started. I was born Stepan—now I'm Steven. Krikor is Kirk, and Haroutoun is Harry. And it began before us, even—Nicky was Nishan—remember?"

"You respect your uncle. He's a wise man. Do you know what he would say?"

"No, I don't know what he would say."

"He would say, 'First you must be free on the inside. Then the outside won't matter.'"

"Not to him, maybe, but to me it will. When I get to high school, I'll be too old to play after the first year. I'll be ineligible because I'll be too old. I'm the best shot on the basketball team, I'm one of the best fielders on the softball team, and next year I'm taking up football. But after junior high school I'm dead. Why would a coach play a sophomore, if that's his last year of eligibility? I want to be free on the outside. Then I'll be free on the inside."

"That's not how it is. Someday you'll understand."

"Someday! Someday! Well, jam it! I'm leaving!"

"Come back for supper," my mother called after me.

"Maybe I will and maybe I won't." I slammed out of the door, hoping the glass would shatter. I got on my bike and rode out to the river. I still had the freedom of my bike. I could still be alone. And the river was always there, waiting, in movement, promising change, promising that life could be different because it didn't always have to be the same.

But how could I change my life? Would I have to change myself? Was that the message contained in what she said was my uncle's formula for freedom? Was anyone free? Could anyone be free? And if not, then why could I think of nothing else? If it wasn't attainable, why did I crave it? Was there anything unattainable that you could have even a thought about? Wasn't thinking just as real as anything else? If I thought something, didn't that make it so? Yes, that's right. Yes, yes, I repeated to myself, that's so, but something's missing! What is it, I asked myself. What is it, I asked the river. Tell me! If anyone knows, you do. You know everything about time. It has to do with time, doesn't it? Yes, of course, it's time, isn't it?

No, not time, the river said, but *in* time.

Yes, *in time!* In time, in time, I repeated, again and again as I looked over the water, wanting more of everything than I knew I could have.

I broke a twig and hurled it into the water, and then another and another, and watched them float away downstream, each one a thought, an idea— but none of them an answer.

And then it came to me. I was holding the broken parts of a twig in my two hands. *It has to be accomplished.* Freedom has to be accomplished. It has to be achieved, realized. Yes, that's it: freedom cannot be given; it can only be earned by my own efforts. Did that make it inner freedom? I wondered. Well, it didn't matter how you defined it.

My mother was half right. It wasn't a free country, but free people could live here. Maybe!

THE GARDEN

Uncle Mihran lived in a small house on La Salle Street. He liked sitting on his back porch, which overlooked the garden he had planted with all of the fruit-bearing trees in Wisconsin that he could find. He enjoyed pruning his trees, grafting different varieties for "experimentation," as he said, and doing whatever repairs the trees required. He called his trees "my children," because, he explained, they would always be dependent on him.

I leaned my bike against the porch and joined my uncle.

"Stepan, it is like this. In the order of *being*, fruit trees are the highest. I am speaking of the tree world now. But fruit trees are delicate, easily hurt, in need of attention and care—tender care—and if

95

abandoned, they soon become wild, food for worms, not for man. Isn't that interesting?"

"Yes, Uncle," I said. I was trying to arrange in my mind all he had told me. "Why don't they teach things like that in school, Uncle?"

"Because in this country they teach from books, and even *about* books, instead of from life and about life. Books instruct, but life teaches."

"What about the good books?" I said. I was thinking of Uncle's books. So far as I knew, he was the only Armenian in town with a library of his own. "Thanks to the Tekeyans, I'm beginning to find good books to read."

"That's it, you see—*you* must find the books that are right for you. In a good school there will be someone to point you in a direction, as the Tekeyans have done in your case. But once you have begun, you must find your own path for yourself—and by yourself. It is no easy matter, but nothing any of us do will ever be more important."

I looked over at Uncle Mihran. He was staring out at his trees, waiting for me to speak.

"I don't know what I want," I said. "I only know what I don't want."

"And what is that?"

"I don't want to live in Racine forever. I don't want to be told what to do by people who don't seem to know what they are doing themselves. Which is mostly everybody, especially the old Armenians. Except for you there aren't any adults I can have a serious conversation with. I'd like to

96

speak to the firemen, and the blacksmith, and people like that, but they don't seem to want to talk to me."

"They don't have to speak to you for you to learn from them," Uncle Mihran said.

"Why is that?"

"Because if they were to teach you what they know, you probably wouldn't be able to learn."

"Why, Uncle?"

"For one thing, you're not sure what you want. For another, you can't receive instruction the way you are. You're too angry."

Uncle Mihran turned away to look at his trees. Two blackbirds were fighting over a plum perched high up in a tree near the garage. "They are coming ripe," Uncle Mihran said. "Everyone wants ripe fruit, but when it is green, eh, then only Uncle Mihran is interested. I care for the green fruit. Everyone else waits for the fruit to ripen. Is that fair?"

"No!"

"No? Are you sure? Life isn't fair, is it? Sometimes, if something suffers over here, something benefits over there. And sometimes these two halves never meet. Maybe they don't even know about each other."

"Do the birds know you are here?"

"Maybe. Maybe not. But the trees know I am here."

"Is that enough?"

"Yes, that's plenty. So what else is bothering you?"

"My mom and dad."

"Yes, of course," Uncle Mihran said, and cupped his chin with his hands. "Just think for a moment. What if you never find your path? What if you find your path and then you lose it or it is taken from you, hah? How would that be? Your parents love you. Maybe not the way you like, but it's their love, given in their way. You see, our paths have been shattered, but now we have the young ones. You are next. You are our future."

"I've heard that before, and that's just it. I don't want to be their future."

"Then be your own future—*make* your own future. It is the same. It is nothing to be angry about."

"What if I don't know what my future is?"

"You are beginning to know already. That is why you are angry, and also why you fight everyone. But don't begrudge. Don't expect others to understand."

"All right," I said, but I wasn't sure I meant it. I wasn't even sure I understood.

"Good," Uncle Mihran said, and turned to look into his garden again. The sun was beginning to set behind the trees. Several birds were dusting themselves in the rows. I understood now why Uncle had kept his garden free of weeds. It was to make a perfect haven for birds. The trees and the garden were as much for them as for the fruit. Uncle sighed, and, without turning to look at me, he said, "Just remember, your mother and father love you."

LILY AND THE SPARROWS

I had graduated from Garfield at last and would now be attending Washington Junior High School. I was about to turn fourteen. Now more than ever I wanted to know what the future held for me.

I was sitting on our front porch, sketching sparrows in my new journal. I had always been intrigued by the family of sparrows that lived inside the towering brick chimney that belonged to the woodwork factory across the street from our house. I was staring at the aperture high up on the chimney that had been made by the removal of one of the bricks. There was one such opening on each side of the chimney. Although they were just ordinary sparrows, their presence in the chimney made them seem magical to me for some reason. It may have been because their homes were visible and yet hidden from view, at a height only they could reach. I wondered now if they weren't reflecting my own life back to me—for I was plain and visible and ordinary, but at the same time I was also secretive and private. But if I was different from others, and separate, it wasn't because I wanted to be or because I tried to be. It was just the way it was. I needed to accept myself—as I was—for that very reason, but it wasn't easy.

I looked up the street and saw Lily walking toward our house. She had taken a job at the J. I. Case office on the corner of State Street and Douglas Avenue, just three blocks away. My mom must have invited her for lunch.

"Making one of your lists?" she asked. "Or are you drawing?"

"I'm not making lists anymore," I said. "I'm trying to describe things with words, but no matter how I try it almost never comes out sounding like my thoughts or feelings. But then every once in a while it *almost* does." I looked up from my notebook, feeling embarrassed and shy. Lily was wearing a kerchief. It was the first time I had seen her with her head covered. The Armenian women all wore funny hats, but their daughters—if they wore anything on their heads—wore kerchiefs. I don't know why it hit me like it did, but in that instant I realized that she would not be going away to music school. It made me wonder if she would stay in Racine for the rest of her life.

She was standing on the sidewalk, trying to decide if she should come in through the front door or go around to the kitchen door on the side, where my mother would be preparing lunch. She said, in a changed tone of voice, "What are you going to do?" I couldn't help but think that she had read my mind.

"I wish I knew," I said. "Tomorrow I go to Washington Junior, but that's not what you mean, is it?"

"No—or rather, yes, that's not what I mean." She laughed and undid the knot under her chin.

"I don't think I want to be an artist, or an architect, or spend all my time in nature as a conservationist, or anything like that. I want to do something that will help me to understand *everything*, and right now I don't understand anything. What good is life if you don't know what it is for?" I stopped speaking and cast my eyes to the sidewalk, feeling self-conscious. But when I looked up at Lily, I saw that she was listening—really listening! I said, "I feel like life is a gift, but that it has to be earned. And I *want* to earn it. Maybe then I will understand what life is for. Do you know what I mean?"

"All too well. You can either feel that way about life, or else you can feel that you are owed. Or maybe that you've been cheated. But neither of those attitudes, or beliefs, will help you to understand, and if that is your aim, well . . ."

"What do you feel?"

"I'm not sure, but I know it is easier to feel cheated or that you are owed. That way you don't have to do anything. And it's hard sometimes not to feel that way. Sooner or later everyone does, if they don't find something to take them away from those thoughts."

"This feeling I have, do you think it comes from me?"

"Does it matter? If you take responsibility for it, then it's yours. That's what matters."

"And if I don't?"

"Then you will lose it. I think that's why some people are bitter. They *become* bitter from not doing what they should do—what *all* humans should do."

"And what is that?"

"You tell me. Or maybe you already have and don't know it."

"How come you know so much, Lily?"

She laughed. "Do I?" She removed her kerchief and shook her hair. After folding her kerchief into a small triangle, she placed it inside her purse. "The more you think about these things, the more you understand—theoretically. But theory isn't interesting; doing is. I know the wrong things. I know what not doing feels like."

I wanted to ask her why she felt that way, but instead I put down my pad in the hope she would continue talking. No adult had ever spoken to me in this way before. With my friends, if I brought up the future, they thought I was crazy. Lily walked up and sat next to me on the porch. I slid over and put my back against the post, so I could look at her face. "I'm ten years older than you, and I was your age when I began to have the kind of thoughts you are having now. You wanted to ask me before why I don't do the things I know to do. I have had to admit to myself that it comes from fear. And also because I consider what others say and think, like my parents, and also the community. Also, I worry. Lots of reasons. I don't think my reasons are very interesting."

I said, "Maybe I'll never find out what I'm good at."

"You have to try. And you have to work at it. It really comes down to effort, doesn't it? We are born with certain possibilities, but we must grow into them through our own efforts and suffering. And if you try, you will see that everything will resist you. Your family, the town, as well as the competition in whatever field you enter. If you can make a force in yourself that is stronger than these obstacles, then their resistance will strengthen you, but if you are weaker than what resists you, then they will weaken you even further. You told me once that none of the arts satisfied you because they each did but one thing. Do you still feel this way?"

"Not exactly," I said, and tried to think. "Some writing, especially poetry, isn't so different from music, except that instead of hearing it only with your ear you also feel it inside—but the feeling is similar because poetry really can be musical."

"What else?"

"When I describe something with words, it's not so different from drawing, because I'm just trying to put down what is there. Whether I use words or line and color really doesn't matter."

"I've always thought a well-constructed book isn't so different from a chair or building. . . ."

"Like architecture," I said.

"Yes, like architecture," Lily said, and smiled.

"I've noticed one other thing about writing. When I write out my problems, I understand them better, because it causes me to line up my thoughts and feelings so I can see them. When I order them in this way, I often see the solution to my problem."

"So maybe writing isn't a compromise for you after all. Also, you can write in private. It can be your secret, and no one need know, because all you need is pencil and paper. Which also means you can travel light." She laughed and started to get up.

Was she telling me that she had tried and then given up? Was that what the look on her face was saying? How had she known that I needed help? She had spoken to me like an adult, and I had understood her like an adult—almost. Maybe I would know better what all of it meant when I grew up. Maybe she was helping me to grow up.

After she had gone inside, I picked up my pad and began sketching again. All at once I felt light inside, and free. I looked up as a sparrow flew straight down from the chimney onto our tiny patch of lawn, which I had recently seeded.

I watched now as the sparrow returned to his chimney home, turning once, twice, before disappearing inside. Someday, I thought to myself, I am going to tell about my sparrows.

GLOSSARY

ahmoht	shameful
basturma	spiced dried beef
choreg	breakfast pastry
Deegen	Mrs.; Madame
jarbeek	enterprising
jeentz	genes
kufta	stuffed meatball of ground lamb, onions, nuts, and spices
madagh	sacrifice; as used here, the name of the annual church picnic
odars	foreigners; non-Armenians
peda	Armenian bread
sarma	pigs in the blanket
yavroos	dear one; my dear
Yegour	Come here
zhkmela monte	small pasta boats with meat stuffing baked and served in a broth with yogurt